Dònal Òg

and

the Fairy Fort

by

Donal McCarthy

Illustrations by Emily Fuhrer

Joshua Tree
Publishing

• Chicago •

Dònal Òg and the Fairy Fort
BOOK ONE OF THE DÒNAL ÒG SERIES

by Donal McCarthy

Published by
Joshua Tree Publishing
• Chicago •
JoshuaTreePublishing.com

13-Digit ISBN: 978-1-956823-03-5

Credits: All Illustrations by Emily Fuhrer

Disclaimer:

Dedication

To my daughters
Cara, Ashling, and Níamh
and my grandaughters
Eden and Aria

Thank You
Emily Fuhrer
Ami on Vancouver Island
John Paul Owles

Dònal Òg and the Fairy Fort

Lying quietly in the long grass, Dònal Òg listened to the hum of the bumblebees as they flew from flower to flower. A lark launched itself high into the sky on flapping wings, soaring until Dònal Òg could barely see it hanging as if suspended.

A rabbit family nibbled on the fresh grass nearby. The young ones were running around playfully until a squeak from their mother brought them to heel. In the meantime, he was building his courage up to undertake a very dangerous move.

"You are a fearless, brave warrior," he told himself.

Da always told him that their McCarthy ancestors were the kings of Munster, the bravest of the brave. (His uncle Séan on his mother's side of the family would mutter that they were probably the stable hands that mucked out from the horses, but everyone ignored him.)

"Tomorrow, you are seven years old, and nothing scares you," Dònal Òg told himself but without much conviction. The source of his very real fears was directly ahead of him.

A large fairy fort loomed on the skyline—a hawthorn tree surrounded by a circle of blackthorn bushes. The warnings of his parents rang loud in his ears: "You are strictly forbidden to enter or go near the fairy fort!" The promise of the severest punishment had been drilled into him since the time he could crawl. The fairies—or little people as they liked to be called (they hated being called fairies)—lived there and would punish those who dared disturb their sacred places with their human presence.

His aunt Tess, the expert in all things to do with the little people, told him that for those who understood fairy lore (such as herself), it was written in large letters using invisible fairy ink: "Humans and other evil-smelling creatures, keep away! Enter here at your own peril! Bid farewell to all those that you love and those that love you!" They promised all sorts of misfortune to those who didn't take heed.

With those kinds of warnings, the local community took them seriously. The farmer who owned the field wouldn't go anywhere near it. If any animal wandered in there, it was left for dead. If ever it came back out (much fatter than when it went in as the grass was longer and sweeter), it was immediately sold to an English settler. They paid a pretty penny for such a fat, sleek beast. It was deemed to be bewitched and could never be accepted back into the herd. As the English were deemed to suffer from the same curse, it was felt that they belonged to each other from then on.

For generations, the humans and the fairies lived more or less in harmony with the other; each honored the agreement to respect each other's territory. Every now and then, a foolish human would decide to hunt for the fairies' golden treasure rumored to be hidden under the trees in the fairy fort. When they awoke outside the fort days later, they could only babble instead of speaking properly. They couldn't remember anything that had happened all the time they were inside. Da was heard muttering that it was too much bad whiskey they were suffering from, but Ma shushed him crossly.

Under normal circumstances, Dònal Òg wouldn't dream of even looking directly at the doomed place, but these weren't normal circumstances. Ma had shooed him out of the house with orders to go and forage for firewood. It was needed to set a fire in the hearth to cook dinner for the family.

His two cousins, Eden and Aria, were visiting for a few weeks. They lived far, far away on the other side of the world. He desperately wanted to show them how brave and strong he was.

He had searched high and low, but little firewood was to be found. He and his siblings had cleared out every hedgerow for miles around. By now, he was desperate. No firewood meant no supper. That meant that everyone would go hungry. He thought he didn't mind for himself (after all, he was nearly seven and grown-up), but the thought of his sister going hungry was more than he could bear. She was his hero, always there to help and soothe him when he needed her. His cousins Eden and Aria would think he was a weakling, not the brave hero that he wanted them to see that he was.

Wood would have to be found, and there, directly ahead of him, was an abundance of dead blackthorn branches. The bushes had been growing there undisturbed for hundreds of years. As branches died and dropped off, they were left to rot—the fairies' curse ensured that.

I could just run in and pick up an armful, he thought to himself. *No one will notice or be any wiser. There is enough wood there to keep the family fire going for months.*

But could he dare gather it up? Would it bring misfortune and calamity to his entire family if he stole from the little people? His heart pounded so hard he thought it might leap out of his chest, then thought how odd it would look if his heart bounded down the meadow without him. He looked around carefully, and he could see the ancient hawthorn tree looking down on him but felt it wished him no harm.

Everyone knew that the hawthorn tree was very special in the eyes of the fairies. It was a beautiful tree of some twenty feet tall, with serrated green leaves and abundant bright, cheerful red berries. In spring, it was covered in beautiful blossoms that seemed to glow with an inner light that was said to be of fairy origin.

Fairies made their wine from the berries, and when they drank it, they would merrily dance all night long as music rang out from the fort. The berries from the blackthorn bush were blue-gray and smoky colored. They had a tart taste when eaten, and when the fairies drank the wine made from these berries, they got very cranky and gloomy. No one wanted to meet them when they were like this. It was much safer to avoid them if possible. It wasn't as difficult as one might think. Just by listening to the music, one could tell immediately what mood they were in. Where possible, each party avoided contact with the other.

The blackbird continued to sing its cheerful song as if to reassure him that all was well in the world and that no harm would befall him if he ventured closer. He decided to wait a little longer. The warnings from Aunt Tess were loud in his ears on how the fairies were always trying to trick humans into believing that they were friendly and then bewitching them when their guard was down. Their favorite trick was to turn one into an animal or insect, such as a goat, donkey, weasel, frog, or daddy longlegs. He often heard Da say that the evil old nanny goat in the yard was his grandmother from his mother's side of the family. He couldn't be sure because the fairies had taken her before he was born. He often thought she must have been a very cross woman; the goat chased them every chance it got.

Just then, a raucous large black crow chased the blackbird away. He was glad he had waited. Everyone knew that the crows were the fairies' watchdogs. They watched when people sowed their crops, then led the fairies there at night to steal the seed. Every chance a farmer got to shoot a crow, he did. Perched high in the hawthorn tree, it glared around malevolently but failed to spot Dònal Òg as he stayed as still as a rock on the ground. Cawing harshly, it flew on to its next watchtower in the distance.

Screwing up his courage, Dònal Òg darted swiftly to the fort and gathered up as much wood as his arms could take. Then he hightailed it home as fast as his legs could carry him. Fearing the fairies would chase him, he uttered a loud shriek and bolted down the hill. Such speed did his fear lend him that he reached his front door long before his loud shriek did.

At the sight of the wood, he received a hero's welcome from his family.

Soon the fire was blazing cheerfully, filling the cottage with warmth and light. The dancing flames cast a warm glow on everyone. Darkness fled into the corners and out under the door. In no time, the large black three-legged cast-iron pot of potatoes was upended on the table. Slabs of yellow salted butter and jugs of fresh cow's milk were added to the feast. Everyone declared that it was the best food they ever had.

By now, Ma was looking worried. She had noticed that the pot was once again full of potatoes. She knew that she hadn't filled it again. Da remarked how long the wood was lasting and what wonderful heat it was giving out.

"Where did you find it, my boy?" he asked Dònal Òg.

"I took it from the fairy fort," Dònal Òg replied.

The silence that followed was so deafening that one could hear the trout in the nearby stream swishing its tail back and forth in the water as it kept its position in the fast-flowing current. The look of horror on both parents' faces frightened him.

What could be wrong with a potato pot that filled itself perpetually and a fire that never needed wood to be added to it? he thought. *Hadn't I fooled the fairies and got away with it?* It wasn't their pot of gold, so they wouldn't be really angry.

(They hated losing any of their gold and would never stop trying until they got it back).

Da and Ma knew otherwise! The pact had been broken, and swift reprisals were sure to follow. Grabbing a bucket of water, Da threw it on the fire to quench the flames, hoping that the smell of the firewood hadn't reached the noses of the fairy folk. The flames disappeared under a cloud of steam and smoke but instantly reappeared as bright and hot as before.

In the midst of all this, a long, baleful face looked in over the half-opened door and let out an unearthly scream. Believing it was a fairy who had come to snatch her youngest child (for fairies loved to steal human children), Ma hurled a pot of hot water at it. (Fairies hated hot water. It made them sneeze, and their skin shriveled, making them look old. They really hated that). With a loud yell, the face quickly disappeared. As the nanny goat beat a hasty retreat down the yard, Da yelled after it: "Serves you right, you cantankerous old witch!" Then he realized with a sigh that his tea would now be delayed since Ma had thrown his tea water out.

In the meantime, Ma was preparing for the coming war with the little people. It was a war that had been fought many times over the centuries. Sometimes the fairies won and demanded treasure in one form or another from the humans. Sometimes it was human children they demanded and, at other times, the milk from the cows and goats. Every night they would suck the animals dry and would leave nothing for the family. But quite often, the humans bested them, and they got to make their demands. It was always just one thing: their pot of gold!

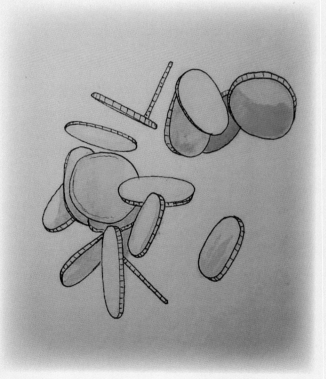

Now the one thing that the fairies loved above all else was gold. They went to the end of the earth to find it and hoarded it once it came into their possession. They buried it deep under the ground beneath the hawthorn tree and wove magic spells to protect it. They would do anything and everything to protect it and keep it in their possession.

One particular spell was for when all was lost and they were about to lose their hoard. It was said that if a human looked directly at the gold, they would go insane. Da often muttered to himself that Ma's people must have seen many pots of gold in their time. Dònal Òg noticed that Da never said it loudly in front of Ma, and he thought it was because Da didn't want to make her sad.

He thought Da was good that way. He also never made Ma sad about her mother being bewitched into the nanny goat.

Humans also had their strategies and secret weapons. The fairies didn't always get their own way. Based on that, Ma knew that the fairies could be persuaded to call a truce if they felt the humans were about to get possession of their gold. First off, Aunt Tess was summoned to the house to manage the coming conflict. In turn, she called on the help of those older women in the community whom she felt would be useful in the battle.

Wars against the fairies were usually run by the womenfolk. It was felt that the men were too hotheaded and could be easily outsmarted by the fairies. Men were considered gullible and easy to hoodwink. That's what the women said. Da muttered that he had never yet met a woman who admitted when she was wrong.

A council was set up when all were present, and each woman took responsibility for various tasks. Each brought with her a special mirror that was used at times like this. It helped them see into the fairie world.

Aunt Tess instructed the children to make small mounds of salt (an eggcup full) in a ring around the cottage, spaced twelve inches apart and six feet away from the walls. Behind each mound (the side nearest the cottage), five thimblefuls of Irish whiskey were placed. It was common knowledge that fairies loved salt. They loved it almost as much as gold. They would gulp it down in vast quantities whenever they found it. This led to a terrible thirst, so they would pour the whiskey down their throats as fast as they could to quench it.

Now the one thing that could knock a fairy out for hours was a sip of good Irish whiskey (no point in giving them Scotch, as it just made them irritable).

Whenever someone gave Da a bottle of Scotch, he would put it in the goats' mash and feed it to the nanny goat. He said that at least it got rid of her ticks.

Once the fairies were knocked out, they must be moved ten feet back from the property (repeat the exercise until sunrise). By then, they should be out of sight of the cottage and would have forgotten their reason for being there. It must be done to perfection; they must believe that they had the best party of their lives. One misstep could undo all the efforts taken so far. Lifting them and placing them in their new positions must be done by children as they were much gentler than adults, who might be tempted to dropkick them into the next parish.

Once the light broke the sky, just a second before dawn, they must return to their homes beneath the hawthorn tree. Exposure to sunlight was disastrous to them. They would lose all their magic powers and could be made servants by the humans. No self-respecting fairy wanted that to happen. Just as the first ray of sunlight painted the morning sky, they disappeared as if they never existed and left the humans wondering if it was all just a dream.

That was the first line of defense, and hopefully, it would all go according to plan. Orders were issued. Measurements were taken, checked, and rechecked. There was too much riding on this for any mistakes to happen. Ma and Aunt Tess were everywhere. There was a minor hiccup when some of the whiskey seemed to have disappeared. Da looked guilty and said he must have missed the fairies slipping past him. Aunt Tess looked skeptical, but nothing more was said. After that, Da paid far more attention. It was very important that the salt and whiskey were placed just as the sun sank below the land in the west—before the fairies could see what was happening (which, of course, the humans didn't want).

However, every good general has a second plan of battle in case the first one doesn't work. Ma was a good general. She knew that appeasement of the angry fairies had to be undertaken even if plan number one worked perfectly. There was no guarantee that they would continue to forget the transgression forever. No, it was important that the fairies were in her debt and felt that they had to give up their gold or bargain their way out of the debt.

The council gathered and put their heads together. There was much discussion back and forth, pots of tea consumed, and loaves of currant cake eaten. Eventually, a plan was agreed on, and action was undertaken to put it in motion when the appropriate time arrived.

At that time of year in Ireland, the sun set very late. As they watched it sink slowly into the Atlantic Ocean, they waited with bated breath. Suddenly, it was time to scramble to get the job done, and such was the thoroughness of Aunt Tess's preparations that everything went off without a hitch. From the fort came the sounds of the fairy flutes as they prepared to issue forth and confront the humans who dared defy their rules and steal their precious property. Down the hill, they advanced to the music of the flute and pipe, spinning and twirling in a blaze of color and light. So merry were they that the children advanced to meet them. Bewitched by the music (for that was the fairies' way), they had to be restrained by the adults and locked inside the cottage, with the menfolk blocking every exit or entrance.

On came the mesmerizing happy music, but now the adults could feel the undertones of sadness and loss, for that would be their lot if they didn't win this battle tonight. Their children would be swept away to live with the fairies forever, never again to be seen by a human eye.

Sometimes before dawn on clear frosty nights, they would hear them calling out to them to come and save them from eternal servitude in an alien world. However, they knew that there was no way back for those who had been taken. No, tonight was not a battle that could be lost.

Suddenly the music ceased, and a loud hurrah was heard. The salt had been discovered by the fairies. Great was the joy of the horde. Here was a treasure beyond their wildest dreams in quantities never seen in the lifetime of the oldest member there. He was 320 fairy years old (or 3,200 in human terms). They devoured the mounds with great speed and then discovered the whiskey. The music once again flowed, and they leaped and twirled until they were overcome by whiskey and exhaustion and sank into a deep slumber.

When all was silent, the children went silently forth and gently lifted each fairy, moving it back to the appointed spot. More mounds of salt were heaped in front of them, this time in greater quantities. The amount of whiskey was also doubled. Moving silently toward the cottage, the children were wide-eyed. They had never seen fairies before. Now they saw that they were not the happy dancing creatures that they imagined to be. They had cold, cruel eyes and thin hooked noses. They oozed malevolence from every pore of their being, and the children were more than happy to disappear back inside the warm cottage.

Once again, as the fairies awoke from their befuddled sleep and discovered the salt, they were overcome with joy. They consumed it all again with gusto with the same results as before. Thrice more that night, the operation was repeated, and then again one time more. Now was the time to set their master plan in motion. If they were to bring the war to an end here tonight, they had to capture the king of the fairies himself and hold him to ransom against the rising sun.

In the last move of the battle, one of the mounds of salt was one hundred times larger than all the others. Such a mound had never ever, ever been seen by the fairy horde. (In human terms, it was about two kilograms.) Definitely a ransom fit for a king. When the king saw it, he was overcome with greed. Instead of sharing it with his people, he decided to eat it all himself. He ate so much that he had to drink even more than before.

As the dawn sky got lighter and lighter, he failed to notice he was in danger. Concentrating as he was, he missed the first pinpricks of light streaking the clouds. His befuddled brain didn't notice Dònal Òg as the boy threw a blanket over the king's head and grabbed him. Screaming and spitting, he threatened all sorts of vile retribution. Dònal Òg lifted the blanket slightly until a sliver of sunlight touched the king's foul skin, and then he threatened to remove the blanket completely if the king didn't cooperate.

The king was in fear of his immortal life. One ray of direct sunlight was all that lay between him and slavery for the rest of his life in the mortal world. His hoard of gold would be lost forever to the humans, his kingdom impoverished, and his people scattered from their fairy fort, where they had lived long before the mortal humans had invaded his world.

Imprinted deep in his tribal memory was the day that their fairy world, as they knew it, had come to an end. In olden times, the fairies had ruled the entire world. It was a life of gaiety. Music rang out from every corner of their land. Food and drink were produced magically, and fairies led enchanted lives.

Then one terrible day, hordes of dark strangers arrived in the land. They were tall and powerful. The fairy magic had no effect on them, for their shields were made of bronze and their spears of iron.

Soon the fairies were defeated and were eventually forced underground to live out their days. There they had rebuilt their lives as best they could. They could no longer tolerate sunlight and lived with fear and hatred in their hearts for the invaders above ground. The king knew he had to get back underground at any cost; he would promise the human anything he asked for and then try to cheat him at the last moment.

Dònal Òg knew all this. Aunt Tess had coached him all night long on the devious ways of the fairy folk. She said, "The secret is never to tell them directly what it is exactly you want. Keep the king in fear and guessing until the very last moment. Only then you should exact a promise from him and let him leave back to his own world still in your debt."

As Dònal Òg was the one who had transgressed, he was the one who had to do the deal with the king. As the hours progressed, he kept hinting different wishes to the king. The one thing he never mentioned was the gold. This caused great tribulation in the king's mind; he knew how much the humans coveted gold. He kept mentioning it, but the human didn't bite.

This distracted him even further. What else could be so important that it outshone gold?

The sun climbed ever higher; its zenith was approaching unless a deal had been struck. By then, it would be too late. Trying to distract Dònal Òg with precious stones and gold had no effect. At nearly seven years old, it meant nothing to him, but the king didn't understand that.

Finally, with less than eleven seconds left, Dònal Òg told the king of his wishes, a lifetime of wood from the fairy fort's hedge and a complete amnesty of hostilities between the fairies and all the people in the district. If the fairies ever broke that promise, he had the right to demand all their gold. They could not renege on a promise made by their king. If they did, their hawthorn tree would be uprooted, and their fort destroyed and plowed under.

With less than half a heartbeat left, the king had to agree. To help make up the king's mind, Dònal Òg lifted the blanket slightly so that the king could feel the sun. With an anguished shout, he called out all the terms of the agreement and swore that both he and all his people would forever be in debt to the humans and live in peace with them. A great shout went up from both sides as the blanket ball soared over the hedge and landed at the base of the hawthorn tree, where the king quickly disappeared underground.

Dònal Òg returned as a hero to his family. His cousins Eden and Aria hugged him and told him what a great man he was. They made him tea and served him many slices of fruit cake. He was very, very happy.

Aunt Tess wasn't well pleased to start with. She had instructed him to secure peace between the fairies and themselves, nothing more. He had added the demand for the firewood himself because he was tired of scouring the hedgerows far and wide when a ready supply was less than five minutes from his front door. He believed that he deserved a present as today was his seventh birthday. What could be better than a present from the high king of the fairies? Especially as he had outsmarted the fellow. No more drudgery or searching for wood in the freezing cold or driving rain. Now that was a life-changing present!

The added benefit of everlasting heat and a pot that refilled itself soon had Ma and Aunt Tess seeing it from his point of view. They quickly forgave him for all the trouble that he had brought upon the family. He had shown that he was brave and resourceful when it was required of him. He beamed with pride and joy. Da hugged him and told him he was a brave man.

He promised himself many more adventures. His epic adventure with the walking trees was soon to follow. But that's a story for another day.

And that is how Dònal Òg became the hero of his people.

The End.

Printed in Great Britain
by Amazon

79336216R10022